ONCE AGAIN, FOR PEGGY - S.J.H.

FOR ALL KINDS OF FAMILIES - M.F.B.

Thanks to Cynthia Bournellis, Pat Kindermann, Lorraine Rader,
David Michael Cunningham and, of course, Peggy Anne Harper
for all your constructive comments and advice.

Published by Inspire Press, Inc.
P.O. Box 33241, Los Gatos, CA 95030

Mary's paintings for this book were done
in watercolor, acrylic, and colored pencil and ink
on hand-printed papers.

ISBN 0-9741800-1-7

Cataloging-in-Publication data
available from publisher

Printed in the United States of America

Manufactured by Phoenix Color Corporation

THE BLACK SHEEP

Story by Stephan J. Harper

Illustrations by Mary FitzGerald Beach

INSPIRE PRESS

Once upon a time there was a black lamb born to a flock of white sheep.

"How unusual," said the mother ewe.

"How very unusual," said her sister.

Even the old ram was surprised when they returned from the lambing grounds to show off the new addition to the family.

But the black lamb was loved as the other lambs were loved and he took his place in the herd. They roamed the country, up the hills and mountainsides and through the valley meadows, grazing where grasses grew tall and sweet. Often they would stop by the river, where the younger sheep played in the shallows under the watchful eyes of their elders.

As the seasons passed, the black lamb grew and sprouted a fine pair of yearling horns that made his mother very proud. But she saw that her black sheep was a little sad when the others started families of their own and he was left alone.

One late summer afternoon, a wolf slipped out of the woods and into the pasture where the sheep were grazing. The flock panicked and took off together in a white cloud. The wolf saw a lone dark spot and raced for the black sheep. The herd scattered. The wolf chased the black sheep through the meadow and back into the woods, where he finally trapped his prey.

The wolf snarled and growled and his sharp teeth made a terrible smile. All the black sheep could do was bleat, H-E-E-E-L-P! H-E-E-E-L-P!

Suddenly, from the rocks nearby leaped the old ram, landing between the black sheep and the wolf. The old ram lowered his head and charged. But the wolf was too quick and the old ram cracked his horns loudly against the rocks. The wolf attacked from behind. The old ram turned and dipped his head and the wolf let out a howl. He was caught by the old ram's horns and tossed high in the air. The wolf dropped with a loud crash into the branches of a fallen tree where he lay still, his breathing faint and shallow.

The old ram and the black sheep returned to the herd and from that day roamed together. The black sheep enjoyed the old ram's stories and longed to have adventures of his own.

"Why am I the only black sheep in the herd?" he asked one day.

"I've never seen a black sheep before you," said the old ram. "When I was young, the elders told a story about a herd of black sheep but..."

"Are they like me?" cried the black sheep.

"It's only a story," continued the old ram. "Legend says they live in the land beyond The Great Forest and are the greatest of all jumpers."

Maybe I'm a great jumper, too, dreamt the black sheep that night.

He could not stop thinking about the black sheep beyond The Great Forest. He wanted to start a family of his own. And it was too dangerous for him to stay with the white herd now. *What will happen the next time the wolf attacks?* he wondered. There was only one thing to do: he would find the black herd.

"The journey will be uncertain and you will face dangers far greater than the wolf," warned the old ram. But the black sheep would not change his mind.

That night he told his mother. "Remember you always have a home here," she said.

The next day he said good-bye to the herd and set out on his quest. For many days and nights he traveled, following the river he knew so well. When he came to The Great Forest, the trees rose up and up, hiding the sky and he felt very small. At night he rested in the unquiet darkness, frightened by the strange sounds and smells.

Rustling leaves woke him early one morning. He heard a twig snap, then a low growl and he jumped up to face the wolf! This time the old ram couldn't help. The black sheep took off through the forest, leaping over fallen branches and big mossy logs still wet with dew. The wolf chased close behind. Faster and faster they ran until the black sheep was almost out of breath. He saw a clearing ahead and a wide ravine beyond. The wolf did not slow his pace.

I am a great jumper, I am a great jumper, said the black sheep to himself; and at the ravine, he jumped. For a moment he was flying.

When he landed on the other side, he turned to see the wolf had jumped, too. But the wolf did not make it across and he fell to the bottom of the ravine. The black sheep ran for a long time afterward and did not look back.

At last he came out of The Great Forest and to the long mountain range just as the old ram had described. The black sheep felt safe among the rocks where he knew his less sure-footed enemies couldn't follow. In the day, he continued over the rocky terrain. At night, snug beneath a craggy outcrop, the black sheep dreamt of the white herd and his home, now far away.

One day he came upon two bear cubs chasing a large pine cone as it wobbled down the smooth rock face. When the cubs saw the black sheep they scampered over, their noses held high, sniffing in curiosity. The black sheep was curious, too, and put his own nose in the air. Suddenly from above came a deafening roar and a large brown bear bounded down the side of the mountain toward the group. Playtime was over and the black sheep bolted, leaving the mother bear with her cubs.

Soon the mountains turned to hills and the valleys became green pastures again, rich in bluegrass. He met the river, winding its way as before.

The black sheep followed in the soft mud of the riverbank and when the river made a sharp turn into the rapids he knew it was time to cross to the other side.

The river's too fast to swim, he thought, seeing the whitewater swirling around the rocks. *And it's too far to jump now.*

The black sheep spotted a tree floating downstream and he thought of a way to cross the river. When the tree drifted by, he jumped on—but when he tried to jump off to the other side, he slipped and fell. All he could do was hold on tightly in the fast moving current. Soon he heard a low thunder in the distance and the black sheep saw the river coming to an end. He was rushing toward a waterfall!

"JUMP!   JUMP!"

He looked up and saw a black ewe running along the bank on other side of the river. The black sheep stood for a moment on unsteady legs and then, with all his strength, he jumped.

"That was close!" said the black ewe.

"I-I-I wasn't sure if I could make it!" stammered the black sheep, still shaking from his narrow escape. He couldn't take his eyes off the black ewe. *Is she from the black herd?* he wondered.

"What were you doing in the middle of the river?" she asked. *Looking for you*, he wanted to say. Instead, he told her about the white herd and the wolf and the old ram's story; about his dark nights in The Great Forest and all the rest that finally brought him to her side of the river.

"How brave you were to face so many dangers and journey so far!" said the black ewe. "Let me show you the rest of the way." And the next morning they reached the long green valley where the black sheep saw that the old ram's story was true after all.

"Come meet my family," said the ewe and together they trotted off to the black herd.

From back in the herd there was a sudden commotion and a loud chorus of bleating.

"Here comes trouble," said the black ewe. "Just keep your head down; my brother leads the flock."

A black ram, not much bigger than the black sheep, broke through to the front and challenged the newcomer. The flock froze. The black ram charged and the fight began.

C-R-R-R-A-C-K!!

The two butted heads again and again until they locked horns. They twisted and turned, straining full against each other. Finally the black sheep threw the black ram to the ground and stood over the black ewe's brother.

The rest of the herd welcomed the black sheep into their fold and after that day the black sheep and the black ewe were never apart.

He and the black ram became close friends and together they watched over the herd.

The black sheep had found his new family and he was happy. He was sure the old ram would be happy for him, too.

The next spring, the black ewe gave birth and to everyone's surprise, the newborn lamb was all white.

"How unusual," said the mother ewe.

Maybe not, thought the black sheep.

And as the black sheep watched the newborn grow, he thought about his first family.

The white lamb soon became a young ram joining the other rams playing in the mountains.

"Why am I the only white sheep, father?" he asked one day.

The black sheep told him the story of the white herd that lives in the land beyond The Great Forest.

But he knew an even better way to answer his son's question.

"I'll show you the way," said the black sheep.
And together, they started out on their journey.